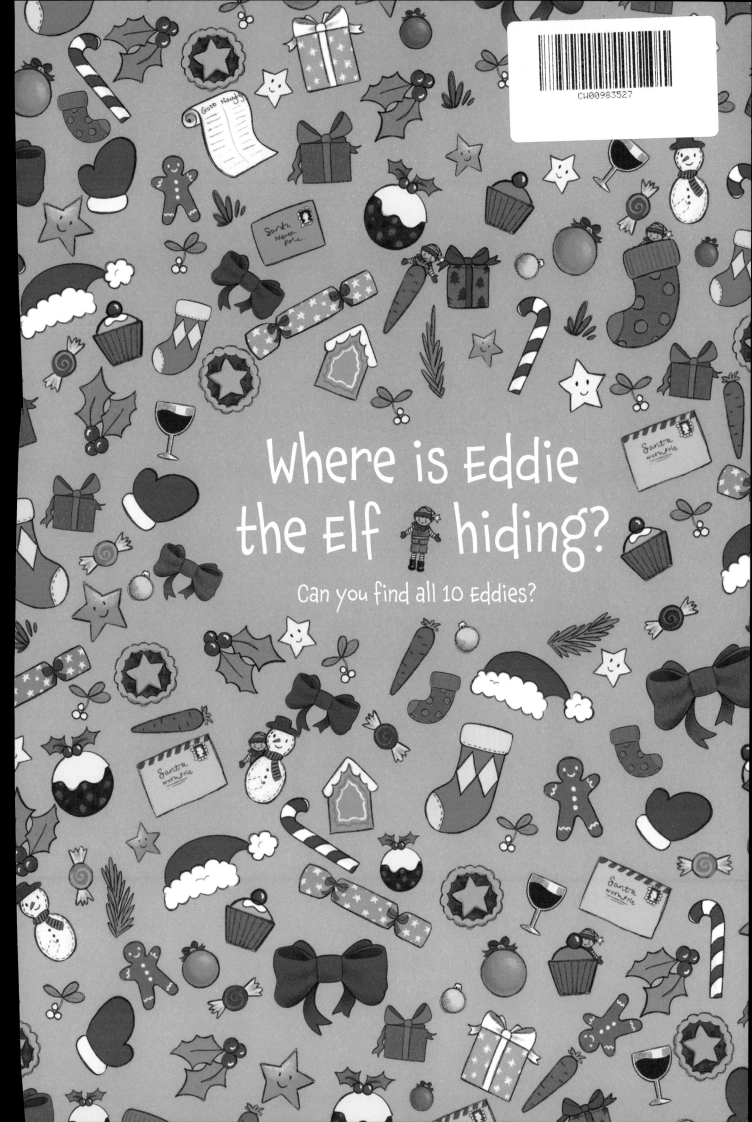

Where is Eddie the Elf hiding?

Can you find all 10 Eddies?

This book belongs to

....

Who are these little gifts for?
Add your own names!

First edition self published and printed by ExWhyZed 2021
Self published by Danielle Verbeeten

Text & Illustrations © Danielle Verbeeten

ISBN: 978 1 3999 0322 6

Eddie the Elf

Written and illustrated by
Danielle Verbeeten

This is for you - Meg, Hazel and Sam
Always believe in Magic!
Love Mum x

This is the story of Eddie the elf,
that lived up high on our kitchen shelf.
His hat was stripy, his waistcoat green,
he had the rosiest cheeks you've ever seen.

ssssssshhhhhhhh!

Now every night in the month of December,
for as many years as I can remember,
while all of our children were sound asleep,
around the house he'd quietly creep.

Every morning he was somewhere new,
on top of the cupboard or grandpa's shoe.
The things he did, they made us laugh,
he gave the cat a bubble bath!

The dog's bowl was his swimming pool,
a midnight dip in doggy drool

eeeeeeeeeeoooo Eddie!

As December came to an end,
we started to worry about our friend.
Christmas had passed, we started to fear it,
Eddie was losing his Christmas spirit!

When January came it was very traumatic,
it was time to put Eddie back up in the attic.

"No," cried Sam "where will he go?
Will he be lonely? How will we know?"
"Don't worry," said Dad "you've nothing to fear,
we'll wrap him up safe, till December this year"

So boxes were packed and the attic room darkened,
but then....

WHOOOOOOSH!
A magical thing happened!

Baubles and teddies all started to sway,
a snowman and stockings all shouted "HOORAY!"
"Wow!" cried Eddie, "how can this be?
a magical party all just for me?"

"Come and look," said the snowman,
"we've a secret to show you,
a magical door we all get to go through.
It's where the elves go, from Jan to November
returning home in time for December!"

"We help Father Christmas and learn to make toys,
compile the list of good girls and boys"
"Wow!" gasped Eddie "I love The North Pole!
and Father Christmas - when can we go?"
"Now!" said the snowman - we'll be back soon!"
So Eddie took a leap of faith and....

Zooooooooom!

Down he flew, as quick as a flash,
landing in the snow with a great big...

crash!

"Hello there Eddie!" Mrs Christmas bent down,
as she smiled and helped him get up from the ground,

"Come meet the elves - they're ever so sweet
and there's one special person I'd like you to meet..."
Eddie was so excited, who do you think it was?

Yep you guessed it...

Father Christmas!

And so the months flew past, as Eddie settled in his home,
for the rest of the year he was never alone.
Christmas drew nearer and the elves were excited,
all was on track - Father Christmas was delighted.

But...

One little elf (called Meg I believe),
had a very naughty trick hidden up her sleeve!

It was too cold around here, Meg the elf felt,
so she changed all the weather to make the snow melt!

Everything turned to chaos
as the temperature began to rise,
riverbanks were bursting,
tiles started to slide.
Gingerbread houses fell to the ground,
and Christmas joy was nowhere to be found!

Everyone was in a panic,
"Meg, what were you doing?"
As they ran around shouting

"Christmas is ruined!"

"No!" cried Eddie, "don't see it this way,
I know we can fix things and save Christmas day.
We still have each other, we'll just work together,
to save The North Pole from the hot sticky weather!"

We'll all work with our talents and strengths,

"Willow spray the glitter, Holly mend the fence!"

"Alice fix the tiles!"

"Hazel make more icing!"

"Max wrap all the presents with ribbons so enticing!"

When they were finished Father Christmas was so pleased,
he was proud of the elves and what they'd achieved.
"Hooray we did it! We achieved our goal,
we worked as a team and saved The North Pole.
We can all return to our families knowing,
that now Christmas Day will be happy and snowing."

But one little elf was sat on her own,
with tears down her cheeks she felt very alone...

"What's wrong?" Eddie asked sitting down in the snow.
"There's nowhere for me to go,
I'm all alone," said Meg the elf,
"I've never had a family shelf!"

"Oh dear," said Eddie "that does sound wrong,
but please don't worry, come along.
Don't feel sad, that's in the past,
we can put things right really fast!
Come home with me and you'll see,
just how happy Christmas can be"

"Oh thank you!," smiled Meg "do you think they'll mind?"
"Come on!," cried Eddie "we've a door to find!"

They bounced along together,
"Father Christmas, see you soon!"
They both took a leap of faith and.....

Zoooooooooom!

Down they flew as quick as a flash,
landing in a box with a great big...

crash!

So now up in the attic on December the 1st,
a cardboard box was waiting to burst.
What was in the box? Can you guess yourself?

Yep! you got it,
TWO elves for the shelf!

And when it's January, the children won't panic,
when it's time to put Eddie and Meg in the attic.

Together they'll travel, through the door they'll go
to visit Father Christmas and their friends in the snow!

The End

But can you find 10 more
Eddies before you go?...